FANTASTIC FUNNY FRIGHTENING

A collection of short stories

Published by Pearson Education Limited, Edinburgh Gate, Harlow, Essex, CM20 2JE.

www.pearsonschools.co.uk

Collection © 2014 Pearson Education Limited

The rights of Terry Jones, Michael Rosen, George Layton, Malorie Blackman, Paul Stewart, Louise Cooper and Jan Mark to be identified as the authors of this work have been asserted by them in accordance with the Copyright, Designs and Patents Act 1988.

This collection first published by Pearson Education Limited as part of Literacy Evolve in 2009. This Wordsmith edition first published in 2014.

17 16 15 14
10 9 8 7 6 5 4 3 2 1

British Library Cataloguing in Publication Data
A catalogue record for this book is available from the British Library

ISBN 978 0 435 16045 6

Printed in Slovakia by Neografia

Acknowledgements

Every effort has been made to contact copyright holders of material reproduced in this book. Any omissions will be rectified in subsequent printings if notice is given to the publishers.

This book is part of Wordsmith.
To order further copies please contact:
Telephone: 0845 630 22 22
Fax: 0845 313 77 77
Email: customer.orders@pearson.com
Web: www.pearsonprimary.co.uk/wordsmith

Contents

The Glass Cupboard

Terry Jones

There was once a cupboard that was made entirely of glass so you could see right into it and right through it. Now, although this cupboard always appeared to be empty, you could always take out whatever you wanted. If you wanted a cool drink, for example, you just opened the cupboard and took one out. Or if you wanted a new pair of shoes, you could always take a pair out of the glass cupboard. Even if you wanted a bag of gold, you just opened up the glass cupboard and took out a bag of gold. The only thing you had to remember was that, whenever you took something *out* of the glass cupboard, you had to put something else back *in*, although nobody quite knew why.

Naturally such a valuable thing as the glass cupboard belonged to a rich and powerful King.

1

One day, the King had to go on a long journey, and while he was gone some thieves broke into the palace and stole the glass cupboard.

'Now we can have anything we want,' they said.

One of the robbers said: 'I want a large bag of gold,' and he opened the glass cupboard and took out a large bag of gold.

Then the second robber said: 'I want two large bags of gold,' and he opened the glass cupboard and took out two large bags of gold.

Then the chief of the robbers said: 'I want three of the biggest bags of gold you've ever seen!' and he opened the glass cupboard and took out three of the biggest bags of gold you've ever seen.

'Hooray!' they said. 'Now we can take out as much gold as we like!'

Well, those three robbers stayed up the whole night, taking bag after bag of gold out of the glass cupboard. But not one of them put anything back in.

In the morning, the chief of the robbers said: 'Soon we shall be the richest three men in the world. But let us go to sleep now, and we can take out more gold tonight.'

So they lay down to sleep. But the first robber could not sleep. He kept thinking: 'If I went to the glass cupboard just *once* more, I'd be even richer than I am now.' So he got up, and went to the cupboard, and took out yet another bag of gold, and then went back to bed.

And the second robber could not sleep either. He kept thinking: 'If I went to the glass cupboard and took out two more bags of gold, I'd be even richer than the others.' So he got up, and went to the cupboard, and took out two more bags of gold, and then went back to bed.

Meanwhile the chief of the robbers could not sleep either. He kept thinking: 'If I went to the glass cupboard and took out three more bags of gold, I'd be the richest of all.' So he got up, and went to the cupboard, and took out three more bags of gold, and then went back to bed.

And then the first robber said to himself: 'What am I doing, lying here sleeping, when I could be getting richer?' So he got up, and started taking more and more bags of gold out of the cupboard.

The second robber heard him and thought: 'What am I doing, lying here sleeping, when he's getting richer than me?' So he got up and joined his companion.

And then the chief of the robbers got up too. 'I can't lie here sleeping,' he said, 'while the other two are both getting richer than me.' So he got up and soon all three were hard at it, taking more and more bags of gold out of the cupboard.

And all that day and all that night not one of them dared to stop for fear that one of his companions would get richer than him. And they carried on all the next day and all the next night. They didn't stop to rest, and they didn't stop to eat, and they didn't even stop to drink. They kept taking out those bags of gold faster and faster and more and more until, at length, they grew faint with lack of sleep and food and drink, but still they did not dare to stop.

All that week and all the next week, and all that month and all that winter, they kept at it, until the chief of the robbers could bear it no longer, and he picked up a hammer and smashed the glass cupboard into a million pieces, and they all three gave a great cry and fell down dead on top of the huge mountain of gold they had taken out of the glass cupboard.

Sometime later the King returned home, and his servants threw themselves on their knees before him, and said: 'Forgive us, Your Majesty, but three wicked robbers have stolen the glass cupboard!'

The King ordered his servants to search the length and breadth of the land. When they found what was left of the glass cupboard, and the three robbers lying dead, they filled sixty great carts with all the gold and took it back to the King. And when the King heard that the glass cupboard was smashed into a million pieces and that the three thieves were dead, he shook his head and said: 'If those thieves had always put something back into the cupboard for every bag of gold they had taken out, they would be alive to this day.' And he ordered his servants to collect all the pieces of the glass cupboard and to melt them down and make them into a globe with all the countries of the world upon it, to remind himself, and others, that the earth is as fragile as that glass cupboard.

7

Water, Water, Water!

Michael Rosen

A man was going along in the desert in Australia when his car suddenly stopped. Nothing he could do would get it to go, so he got out and started to walk. He walked and he walked and he walked and soon he was feeling terribly, terribly thirsty. Finally he saw, coming into view, a little old shack by the side of the road. He staggered up to the door and shouted, 'Water, water, water.'

A man popped his head out the window and said, 'Sorry pal, I only sell ties.'

So the man walked on. And he walked and he walked and he walked.

By now his mouth was completely dried up. Then, coming into view, he saw another little old shack by the side of the road. He staggered up to the door and shouted, 'Water, water, water.'

A man popped his head out the
window and said, 'Sorry pal, I only
sell ties.'

So the man walked on.

Finally he couldn't walk any more, so he crawled. He
crawled and he crawled and he crawled till, coming into
view, he saw a hotel. There by the side of the road, right
in the middle of the desert, was the Hotel Splendid. And
a really splendid hotel it was, with a man in uniform

9

standing on the steps outside.

The man crawled up to the steps and gasped, 'At last. Water, water, water.'

And the man in uniform said, 'Sorry pal, you can't come in here dressed like that. You're not wearing a tie.'

Thank Goodness!

Michael Rosen

There was this man, and he bought a horse, and he jumped on it and said, 'GIDDYUP!' But the horse wouldn't move. So he said, 'How do you make this horse go?'

And the man selling the horse said, 'You say, "Thank goodness".'

'And how do you get it to stop?' asked the man.

And the man selling the horse said, 'You say, "Belly button".'

So off went the man on the horse.

But the horse started going faster and faster, and the man started getting scared because he knew where the horse was taking him – right up to the edge of a Huge Cliff!

'Oh no,' he thought, 'I've forgotten how to get the horse to stop. What am I supposed to say? Oooooh, what is it?'

And the horse was getting nearer and nearer ...

'What's the word? Oh, no ...'

And the horse was right up to the edge ... and he remembered.

He shouted, 'BELLY-BUTTON!'

And the horse stopped.

'Phew,' said the man. 'Thank goodness.' And the horse went whooooosh, straight over the edge.

The Balaclava Story

George Layton

Tony and Barry both had one. I reckon half the kids in our class had one. But I didn't. My mum wouldn't even listen to me.

'You're not having a balaclava! What do you want a balaclava for in the middle of summer?'

I must've told her about ten times why I wanted a balaclava.

'I want one so's I can join the Balaclava Boys ... '

'Go and wash your hands for tea, and don't be so silly.'

She turned away from me to lay the table, so I put the curse of the middle finger on her. This was pointing both your middle fingers at somebody when they weren't looking. Tony had started it when Miss Taylor gave him a hundred lines for flicking paper pellets at

Jennifer Greenwood. He had to write out a hundred times: 'I must not fire missiles because it is dangerous and liable to cause damage to someone's eye.'

Tony tried to tell Miss Taylor that he hadn't fired a missile, he'd just flicked a paper pellet, but she threw a piece of chalk at him and told him to shut up.

'Don't just stand there – wash your hands.'

'Eh?'

'Don't say "eh", say "pardon".'

'What?'

'Just hurry up, and make sure the dirt comes off in the water, and not on the towel, do you hear?'

Ooh, my mum. She didn't half go on sometimes.

'I don't know what you get up to at school. How do you get so dirty?'

I knew exactly the kind of balaclava I wanted. One just like Tony's, a sort of yellowy-brown. His dad had given it to him because of his earache. Mind you, he didn't like wearing it at first. At school he'd given it to

Barry to wear and got it back before home-time. But all
the other lads started asking if they could have a wear
of it, so Tony took it back and said from then on nobody
but him could wear it, not even Barry. Barry told him he
wasn't bothered because he was going to get a balaclava
of his own, and so did some of the other lads. And that's
how it started – the Balaclava Boys.

It wasn't a gang really. I mean they didn't have meetings
or anything like that. They just went around together
wearing their balaclavas, and if you didn't have one you
couldn't go around with them. Tony and Barry were my
best friends, but because I didn't have a balaclava, they
wouldn't let me go round with them. I tried.

'Aw, go on, Barry, let us walk round with you.'

'No, you can't. You're not a Balaclava Boy.'

'Aw, go on.'

'No.'

'Please.'

I don't know why I wanted to walk round with them

anyway. All they did was wander up and down the playground dressed in their rotten balaclavas. It was daft.

'Go on, Barry, be a sport.'

'I've told you. You're not a Balaclava Boy. You've got to have a balaclava. If you get one, you can join.'

'But I can't, Barry. My mum won't let me have one.'

'Hard luck.'

'You're rotten.'

Then he went off with the others. I wasn't half fed up. All my friends were in the Balaclava Boys. All the lads in my class except me. Wasn't fair. The bell went for the next lesson – ooh heck, handicraft with the Miseryguts Garnett – then it was home-time. All the Balaclava Boys were going in and I followed them.

'Hey, Tony, do you want to go down the woods after school?'

'No, I'm going round with the Balaclava Boys.'

'Oh.'

Blooming Balaclava Boys. Why wouldn't *my mum* buy

me a balaclava? Didn't she realize that I was losing all my friends, and just because she wouldn't buy me one?

'Eh, Tony, we can go goose-gogging – you know, by those great gooseberry bushes at the other end of the woods.'

'I've told you, I can't.'

'Yes, I know, but I thought you might want to go goose-gogging.'

'Well, I would, but I can't.'

I wondered if Barry would be going as well.

'Is Barry going round with the Balaclava Boys an' all?'

'Course he is.'

'Oh.'

Blooming balaclavas. I wish they'd never been invented.

'Why won't your mum get you one?'

'I don't know. She says it's daft wearing a balaclava in the middle of summer. She won't let me have one.'

'I found mine at home up in our attic.'

Tony unwrapped some chewing gum and asked me

if I wanted a piece.

'No thanks.' I'd've only had to wrap it in my handkerchief once we got in the classroom. You couldn't get away with anything with Mr Garnett.

'Hey, maybe you could find one in your attic.'

For a minute I wasn't sure what he was talking about.

'Find what?'

'A balaclava.'

'No, we haven't even got an attic.'

I didn't half find handicraft class boring. All that mucking about with compasses and rulers. Or else it was weaving, and you got all tangled up with balls of wool. I was just no good at handicraft and Mr Garnett agreed with me. Today was worse than ever. We were painting pictures and we had to call it 'My Favourite Story'. Tony was painting *Noddy in Toyland.* I told him he'd get into trouble.

'Garnett'll do you.'

'Why? It's my favourite story.'

'Yes, but I don't think he'll believe you.'

Tony looked ever so hurt.

'But honest. It's my favourite story. Anyway what are you doing?'

He leaned over to have a look at my favourite story.

'Have you read it, Tony?'

'I don't know. What is it?'

'It's *Robinson Crusoe*, what do you think it is?'

He just looked at my painting.

'Oh, I see it now. Oh yes, I get it now. I couldn't make it out for a minute. Oh yes, there's Man Friday behind him.'

'Get your finger off, it's still wet. And that isn't Man Friday, it's a coconut tree. And you've smudged it.'

We were using some stuff called poster paint, and I got covered in it. I was getting it everywhere, so I asked Mr Garnett if I could go for a wash. He gets annoyed when you ask to be excused, but he could see I'd got it all over my hands, so he said I could go, but told me to be quick.

The washbasins were in the boys' cloakroom just outside the main hall. I got most of the paint off and as I was drying my hands, that's when it happened. I don't know what came over me. As soon as I saw that balaclava lying there on the floor, I decided to pinch it. I couldn't help it. I just knew that this was my only chance. I've never pinched anything before – I don't think I have – but I didn't think of this as ... well ... I don't even like saying it, but ... well, stealing. I just did it.

I picked it up, went to my coat, and put it in the pocket. At least I tried to put it in the pocket but it bulged out, so I pushed it down the inside of the sleeve. My head was throbbing, and even though I'd just dried my hands, they were all wet from sweating. If only I'd thought a bit first. But it all happened so quickly. I went back to the classroom, and as I was going in I began to realize what I'd done. I'd *stolen* a balaclava. I didn't even know whose it was, but as I stood in the doorway I couldn't believe I'd done it. If only I could go back.

In fact I thought I would but then Mr Garnett told me to hurry up and sit down. As I was going back to my desk I felt as if all the lads knew what I'd done. How could they? Maybe somebody had seen me. No! Yes! How *could* they? They could. Of course they couldn't. No, course not. What if they did though? Oh heck.

I thought home-time would never come but when the bell did ring I got out as quick as I could. I was going to put the balaclava back before anybody noticed; but as I got to the cloakroom I heard Norbert Lightowler shout

out that someone had pinched his balaclava. Nobody took much notice, thank goodness, and I heard Tony say to him that he'd most likely lost it. Norbert said he hadn't but he went off to make sure it wasn't in the classroom.

I tried to be all casual and took my coat, but I didn't dare put it on in case the balaclava popped out of the sleeve. I said tarah to Tony.

'Tarah, Tony, see you tomorrow.'

'Yeh, tarah.'

Oh, it was good to get out in the open air. I couldn't wait to get home and get rid of that blooming balaclava. Why had I gone and done a stupid thing like that? Norbert Lightowler was sure to report it to the Headmaster, and there'd be an announcement about it at morning assembly and the culprit would be asked to own up. I was running home as fast as I could. I wanted to stop and take out the balaclava and chuck it away, but I didn't dare. The faster I ran, the faster my head was filled with thoughts. I could give it back to Norbert. You know, say I'd taken it by mistake. No, he'd never believe me. None of the lads would believe me. Everybody knew how much I wanted to be a Balaclava Boy. I'd have to get rid of the blooming thing as fast as I could.

My mum wasn't back from work when I got home, thank goodness, so as soon as I shut the front door, I put my hand down the sleeve of my coat for the balaclava. There was nothing there. That was funny, I was sure I'd put it down that sleeve. I tried down the other sleeve, and there was still nothing there. Maybe I'd got the wrong coat. No, it was my coat all right. Oh, blimey, I must've lost it while I was running home. I was glad in a way. I was going to have to get rid of it, now it was gone. I only hoped nobody had seen it drop out, but, oh, I was glad to be rid of it. Mind you, I was dreading going to school next morning. Norbert'll probably have reported it by now. Well, I wasn't going to own up. I didn't mind the cane, it wasn't that, but if you owned up, you had to go up on the stage in front of the whole school. Well, I was going to forget about it now and nobody would ever know that I'd pinched that blooming lousy balaclava.

I started to do my homework, but I couldn't concentrate. I kept thinking about assembly next morning. What if I went all red and everybody else noticed? They'd know I'd pinched it then. I tried to think about other things, nice things. I thought about bed. I just wanted to go to sleep. To go to bed and sleep. Then I thought about my mum; what she'd say if she knew I'd been stealing. But I still couldn't forget about assembly next day. I went into the kitchen and peeled some potatoes for my mum. She was ever so pleased when she came in from work and said I must've known she'd brought me a present.

'Oh, thanks. What've you got me?'

She gave me a paper bag and when I opened it I couldn't believe my eyes – a blooming balaclava.

'There you are, now you won't be left out and you can

stop making my life a misery.'

'Thanks, Mum.'

If only my mum knew she was making *my* life a misery. The balaclava she'd bought me was just like the one I'd pinched. I felt sick. I didn't want it. I couldn't wear it now. If I did, everybody would say it was Norbert Lightowler's.

Even if they didn't, I just couldn't wear it. I wouldn't feel it was mine. I had to get rid of it. I went outside and put it down the lavatory. I had to pull the chain three times before it went away. It's a good job we've got an outside lavatory or else my mum would have wondered what was wrong with me.

I could hardly eat my tea.

'What's wrong with you? Aren't you hungry?'

'No, not much.'

'What've you been eating? You've been eating sweets, haven't you?'

'No, I don't feel hungry.'

'Don't you feel well?'

'I'm all right.'

I wasn't, I felt terrible. I told my mum I was going upstairs to work on my model aeroplane.

'Well, it's my bingo night, so make yourself some cocoa before you go to bed.'

I went upstairs to bed, and after a while I fell asleep.

The last thing I remember was a big balaclava, with a smiling face, and it was the Headmaster's face.

I was scared stiff when I went to school next morning. In assembly it seemed different. All the boys were looking at me. Norbert Lightowler pushed past and didn't say anything. When prayers finished I just stood there waiting for the Headmaster to ask for the culprit to own up, but he was talking about the school fete. And then he said he had something very important to announce and I could feel myself going red. My ears were burning like anything and I was going hot and cold both at the same time.

'I'm very pleased to announce that the school football team has won the inter-league cup ... '

And that was the end of assembly, except that we were told to go and play in the schoolyard until we were called in, because there was a teachers' meeting. I couldn't understand why I hadn't been found out yet, but I still didn't feel any better, I'd probably be called to the Headmaster's room later on.

I went out into the yard. Everybody was happy because we were having extra playtime. I could see all the Balaclava Boys going round together. Then I saw Norbert Lightowler was one of them. I couldn't be sure it was Norbert because he had a balaclava on, so I had to go up close to him. Yes, it was Norbert. He must have bought a new balaclava that morning.

'Have you bought a new one then, Norbert?'

'Y'what?'

'You've bought a new balaclava, have you?'

'What are you talking about?'

'Your balaclava. You've got a new balaclava, haven't you?'

'No, I never lost it at all. Some fool had shoved it down the sleeve of my raincoat.'

Peacemaker

Malorie Blackman

'Michela Corbin, what did I just say?'

The class began to snigger. I looked up, dismayed. There, right in front of my desk, stood Teacher Faber. I hadn't seen her coming! I tried to cover my literature screen with my hand but the teacher was too quick for me. She snatched up my screen and started to read the story I'd been writing.

'Michela Corbin, you're supposed to be writing an essay on Section 415 of the Peace Treaty between the Alliance and the Inthral Sector. Not this ... this ... this!'

'I'm sorry. I'll erase it.' I grabbed for my screen. Teacher Faber snatched it back.

'Let us take a look at what has so captured your attention,' said the teacher sarcastically. '... I spun around, quick as a Pogett snake. Davin lunged at me with her laz-sword. Immediately I swung my weapon down to parry her thrust. The sound of laser beam on laser beam zinged almost musically. With a furious roar, Davin whipped her laz-sword upwards towards my head. I ducked and stepped back simultaneously. I didn't want to hurt her but one touch from the laz-sword was lethal – and I wasn't about to die. I ...' Teacher Faber stopped reading, but not before my face was on fire.

'This tish-tosh is dangerous nonsense. I told you the last time that you'd had your final warning. Now you'll go on report – again!' said Teacher Faber with satisfaction. 'And I shall make sure that your mother sees this ... this story of yours.'

My blood ran icy cold. 'My mother will go nuts! I'll do the essay. I'll stay behind and work late. Oh please, you can't ...'

'Watch me,' said Teacher Faber. 'I don't know what's

wrong with you, Michela. You persist with writing these kinds of stories.'

'They're adventure stories,' I protested. 'They're just fiction.'

'You humans are supposed to abhor violence of any kind – even in stories,' said Teacher Faber. 'And yet, Michela, you insist on reading forbidden books like *Treasure Island* and *The Three Musketeers*, and on writing this kind of fantastical, dangerous foolishness.'

It wasn't my fault I read forbidden books. If they weren't forbidden in the first place, then I wouldn't get into trouble for reading them! Mother owned an impressive collection of nineteenth and twentieth-century fiction books, most of them now classified as forbidden. I'd been caught with Mother's books more than once and Mother threatened to burn them all if I was caught with just one of them again. So instead of reading them, I'd taken to writing my own – but that seemed to get me into even worse trouble!

'I won't read or write any more,' I pleaded. 'Please don't report me.'

Teacher Faber keyed in some commands on the console that was situated on her stomach.

'It is done.' Teacher Faber moved away. 'A full report has been transmitted to your mother.'

I scowled at her. Rotten, Pogett-brained, Valunian weasel! I groaned. What was my mother going to say?

'Teacher Faber sent me yet another demerit report on you today.'

'Mother, I can explain ...'

Mother flopped down into her favourite recliner and kicked off her shoes. 'Michela, I don't want to hear it,' she sighed. 'I've reasoned with you, pleaded with you, argued until I'm blue.'

'It was only a story, Mother,' I said quietly.

'A story! Why can't you write stories about proper subjects? What's wrong with peace and diplomacy and friendship? Why must you revel in violence?'

'I don't,' I said furiously. 'They're only stories, Mother ...'

'They're a way of thinking. They're a way of being,' my mother replied. 'You persist in embarrassing me in front of my colleagues. Think of what your father would say if he was still alive.'

And with that one single argument, Mother forced me to shut up and not argue.

An uncomfortable silence filled the room.

'Michela, have you been recoding your Peacemaker?'

'Of course not!' I blustered.

After the 'Treasure Island' incident, I'd been sent to Doctor Bevan to have my Peacemaker checked out. Everyone had a Peacemaker permanently attached to the inside of their left wrist on their eleventh birthday. The Peacemaker was a small, grey disk which looked like one of those old-fashioned buttons people used to use to fasten their clothes. Doctor Bevan explained that it was a behavioural inhibitor – supposed to ensure that the non-aggression we'd all been taught for the last century was more than just a lesson. The Peacemaker was supposed to make sure that it was physically impossible for us humans to be aggressive. No more wars, no more fights, we couldn't hurt each other any more.

Only it didn't stop there. Books and films that had once been considered classics had now been banned. And more and more things these days were taken as signs of belligerence, like talking, laughing and singing too loudly – and as I do all three, I'm constantly on report!

And that was the problem really. I was always letting Mother down – and we both knew it.

Mother shook her head sadly. 'Why do you do it? I read your story, Michela. Is that really what's in your head – in spite of everything I've tried to teach you?

'It was just a story, Mother,' I whispered unhappily.

'And the part where you were fighting with the laz-sword?' Mother asked.

'I put that in because it's the only weapon I've seen a hologram of,' I said.

'You told me that you wanted to train in Je-kan-ia for the exercise, to teach you balance and co-ordination. It's obvious what's in your mind as you use the Kan-ia – you pretend it's a real weapon instead of the plastic stick it is. I forbid you to practise that so-called sport in the future,' said Mother.

'But it's the only thing I'm any good at,' I protested. Don't take that away from me. Not that as well, I thought desperately. But from the look on Mother's face, I knew she really meant it.

'And you can go to Doctor Bevan right this minute and get your Peacemaker checked out. And if you have been tampering with it ...'

'CON ONE! CON ONE! Captain Corbin to the bridge immediately. Captain Corbin to the bridge.'

Mother was interrupted in mid-sentence. She slipped her shoes back on to her feet and within seconds she was out the door. I stared after her. What was going on? What had happened to take us from Condition Four – our usual state – to Condition One, which was only used for extreme, imminent danger?

I was used to Mother, as captain of the ship, being called away at a moment's notice. At first it'd seemed exciting to have such an important mother – captain of the *Kitabu*, one of the most prestigious ships in the Alliance fleet. Recently the excitement had faded away to leave something else, something less noble, in its place. I hardly ever saw her. And it seemed to me that Mother was always Captain Corbin first and being my mother came a long way down the list. I didn't want to feel the way I did, but I couldn't help it.

'Come on, Michela.' I muttered, trying to pull myself together. What should I do now? I glanced down at my Peacemaker. Whatever the emergency was, it'd save me from getting into real trouble.

There was only one way to find out what was going

on. I left the room and headed up to the bridge. Maybe I could sneak in without Mother seeing me.

But the moment I stepped on to the bridge, I gasped, then froze. There, directly in front of the *Kitabu* was the biggest ship I'd ever seen. Only a small portion of it filled the entire viewscreen. It must have had some kind of sensor-jamming device to appear before us like this without any warning.

There was no way anyone would throw me off the bridge. All eyes were on the colossal ship before us.

'Ensign Natsua, activate the universal decoder. Open a channel,' Mother said. She was sitting before the viewer on the bridge, her face solemn. 'This is Captain Corbin of the Alliance ship, *Kitabu*. We come in peace. Our mission is to negotiate trade and route lines through this sector. Do you understand?'

Each encounter with a new alien species called for Mother to issue a similar blurb. The idea was that the alien ship would analyse the words spoken, so that any further communication to them could be translated. That's the way our universal decoder worked as well.

After only a few minutes, the face and upper body of one of the alien crew appeared on the viewer. And such a face as I'd never seen before. My breath caught in my throat and refused to budge. The alien's face held only one eye in what was presumably its forehead. Its nose dominated its face, moving in a series of ridges downwards and outwards. It had lips – different from humans' but similar enough to be recognizable as such. But the thing that made me stare without blinking and turned my stomach over was the alien's skin. It was transparent. I could see grey liquid running through tiny canals in its body. I could see the tops of two organs, one on either side of its upper body, contracting and expanding. The two organs had to be the alien's hearts. The whole thing looked strange, bizarre – and totally disgusting!

'This is Captain Corbin of the Alliance ship, *Kitabu*.

We come in peace. Do you understand?' Mother repeated.

'I am Fflqa-Tur, a Chamrah knight. And I understand perfectly,' the alien replied. 'You have entered our sector without permission and must pay the price.'

'The price?' Mother questioned sharply.

'Our ships are now at war,' said Fflqa-Tur.

'We were not aware that permission was required. My ship is the first Alliance ship to enter this sector. We in the Alliance are peaceful, non-confrontational. We meant no harm.'

'Harm or not, it is Chamrah law. We are now at war.'

'We will not fight you.'

'You have no choice,' said the alien.

'We are prepared to leave this sector and never return,' said Mother.

'You cannot retreat,' Fflqa-Tur said. 'Your path lies ahead'.

Silence.

'Comms down,' Mother instructed the ensign. That way she could hear what Fflqa-Tur had to say but not vice versa.

'Lieutenant Dopp, what's the maximum speed of Fflqa- Tur's vessel?'

'Vel Five, according to our sensors,' the navigation officer replied.

'Comms up,' Mother ordered, to resume two-way communication. 'Fflqa-Tur, I must repeat, we in the Alliance are peace-loving. We will not fight with you. Our ship can travel at more than twice the speed of your craft. I am prepared to use that speed to withdraw so that our meeting does not end in violence.'

'Run if you must,' said Fflqa-Tur. 'But I will spend the rest of my days searching for you throughout the galaxy. The challenge has been issued. It is not yours to reject.'

'But this makes no sense. Why won't you let us leave?

Why must we fight?' Mother asked, an edge creeping into her voice.

'It is our way. And if you leave, not only will our two ships be at war, but my people on Chamrah will be at war with your so-called Alliance,' said Fflqa-Tur. There was a pause before he added, 'I am also bound to inform you of an alternative option, as you did not deliberately break our laws.'

'I'm listening,' Mother said eagerly.

'You may send over your champion to fight against the best knight on my ship,' said Fflqa-Tur.

Mother's shoulders slumped momentarily. 'We have many champions – but not of fighting. Never of fighting.'

'Then how do you propose that we proceed with our combat?' asked Fflqa-Tur.

'As far as I'm concerned, we don't proceed at all. No one on this ship will fight you. It's against everything we believe in.'

Mother began to finger the necklace that Father had given her years before. It was her only sign of nervousness. I could almost hear her thinking, her expression was so intent. 'I have an alternative of my own to suggest.'

'Proceed,' the alien barked.

'We surrender,' Mother said seriously.

No one on the bridge moved. Fflqa-Tur's expression was unreadable and as immovable as an Earth monolith. He beckoned to one of his own bridge crew, and they whispered together for a few moments.

Fflqa-Tur turned back to the viewer.

'We are unfamiliar with the word "surrender". Explain.'

'It means concede defeat, we submit, we yield. We will give ourselves over to you,' Mother said. 'We will not fight.'

Fflqa-Tur smiled. 'Your Alliance is worthless. A Chamrah baby has more courage, more valour. You will stand and fight. Or you will stand and die. The choice is yours. You have fifty locshans to prepare.'

Fflqa-Tur's image disappeared from the viewer to be replaced by his ship.

'Locshans?' asked Mother.

'A moment, Captain,' said Lieutenant Dopp. Silence reigned for several seconds as the lieutenant manually keyed into the universal decoder. 'Fifty locshans would appear to be the equivalent of ten Earth minutes.'

'Ensign, open another channel. I've got to try and reason with them,' said Mother after a pause.

'They're not responding, Captain,' said the ensign.

'Keep trying.' Mother went back to her seat.

'What do we do, Captain?' asked the ensign.

'If they don't answer ... we prepare to die,' Mother said, still staring at the viewer. 'We will not endanger the Alliance. We will not fight.'

'We could leave this sector,' suggested the ensign.

'No, we're not going to run,' said Mother. 'I'm not

going to let this escalate into a full-blown war between the Alliance and the Chamrah nation. We must try to get through to them, but if not ...'

Mother didn't say any more, she didn't have to.

I stared at her. Would she really let us all die, without even a fight? Looking around the bridge, everyone wore the same expression as Mother on their faces. I had my answer.

I looked down at my Peacemaker. How I wished I hadn't tampered with it. The others on the bridge were obviously prepared to do as Mother had said and die rather than go against their beliefs. Me? I wanted to fight. And the feeling was so strong that it scared me. What could I do? I was only thirteen.

'Mother, can I...?' I began.

Mother's head whipped around. 'Michela, get off the bridge. You're not supposed to be up here.' She didn't even let me finish.

I looked at her. She looked at me, worry and

resignation on her face. And at that moment, I knew it was hopeless. We were going to die. I turned away. Unexpectedly, Mother called me back and hugged me.

'Go to our quarters,' Mother said gently. 'I'll join you later.'

After a pause, I left the bridge without another word – but it wasn't to go back to our quarters. It was too late to wonder what I would've done and how I would've felt if I hadn't tampered with my Peacemaker. The point was, I had. And if Fflqa-Tur of the Chamrah wanted a fighter, he would get one.

'Shuttle pod three, you are ordered to identify yourself.' My mother's voice echoed all around the small shuttle pod.

I didn't answer. I couldn't answer – not yet. Not until I had finished rejigging the remote control codes and the forcefield cycle. Once that was one, I opened a channel to the alien ship.

'This is shuttle pod three. I wish to speak to Fflqa-Tur'. I kept repeating the message.

'Michela? What do you think you're doing?' Mother's face appeared on the shuttle pod viewer to my right. Her expression was incredulous, her voice furious. 'Michela. bring that shuttle pod back to this ship at once.'

'I can't Mother. Please don't try to stop me,' I said.

'Ensign Natsua, lock on to that shuttle pod and bring it back,' Mother commanded.

'I can't, Captain. The remote control codes have been changed. We can no longer control that pod,' the ensign replied.

'Then use the tractor beam to bring her back,' Mother snapped.

'Sorry, Captain,' the ensign replied after a few moments. 'The pod's forcefield frequency has been recalibrated. I can't get a lock.'

'Michela, bring that pod back now and I promise we'll say no more about it. Running away from this ship isn't the answer. Your pod can't outrun the Chamrah. Your place is on this ship – no matter what happens,' said Mother.

I stared at her. I couldn't believe it. Did she really think I was trying to run away, to escape the *Kitabu's* inevitable fate? Is that what she really thought of me?

'Bye, Mother,' I said quietly, and I switched off the viewer. I carried on sending out my hailing message to Fflqa-Tur.

Without warning his image appeared on my viewer. I swallowed hard.

'Fflqa-Tur.' I coughed to clear my throat. 'Fflqa-Tur, I am Michela Corbin of the Alliance ship, *Kitabu*. I have come to accept your challenge.'

Fflqa-Tur's eye narrowed, 'You are a human?'

'Yes.'

'You are a knight?'

'Not as such.'

'You are a warrior.'

'Not quite. But it doesn't matter what I am. I'm accepting your challenge,' I said.

There was a deathly hush. Then came a moment when every part of me, every drop of blood in my body, froze, as if I had been suddenly plunged into a bath of liquid nitrogen. The next thing I knew I was standing directly in front of Fflqa-Tur.

'W-what happened?' I whispered.

Fflqa-Tur spoke to me but I didn't understand. I shook my head. Someone behind him came up to me and injected something into my ear. It was uncomfortable for a moment but it didn't hurt.

'You have been brought aboard our ship via our conveyor beam.' Fflqa-Tur spoke and this time I could understand every word. 'I wanted to see you for myself.'

'Well, here I am. What happens now?' I asked.

I felt so strange, so calm. For the first time, the enormity of what I was doing struck me. I was actually doing this. And unlike in one of my stories, I wouldn't be coming back. I'd never see my Mother or the *Kitabu* crew again, but they would be safe and free.

And, as consolation, I was in the middle of an adventure. This was real. Not a fantasy I'd written. Not a dream in my head. Real.

'You will fight against the champion knight of my ship,' said Fflqa-Tur.

'Are you the captain of this ship?' I asked.

'I am.'

'Then I will fight against no one but you,' I said quietly.

Fflqa-Tur stared at me. Then he started to smile. I wondered if the look on his face meant that he was impressed, although for all I knew it could have been indigestion.

'Your challenge is accepted,' said Fflqa-Tur. 'Let us go to the arena.'

'One last thing.' I swallowed hard, afraid I was pushing my luck. 'I'd like our fight relayed back to the

Kitabu. I want my ... Captain Corbin and everyone else on the *Kitabu* to see our contest.'

'Agreed,' said Fflqa-Tur. 'You will now come with me. You will be clothed as a Chamrah knight and you must select your weapon.'

The arena was a small circular pit only about five meters in diameter and filled with what felt like Earth sand, only dark green in colour. Others like Fflqa-Tur sat around the arena. Funny, but they didn't look so disgusting any more. In fact they looked noble. I supposed that, given time – and the right frame of mind – you could get used to anything.

Shouts and cheers filled the air. In walked Fflqa-Tur. He was clothed as I was, in a neck-to-toe outfit that resembled an Earth-England medieval suit of armour, but the Chamrah version was almost transparent, very light and comfortable. In his hand Fflqa-Tur had what looked like a pendulum on a sick. For my weapon, I'd chosen the closest thing to a laz-sword I could find. This one was more primitive – solid metal but with a laser-sharp edge. It wouldn't have made much difference what I'd chosen really. I had never faced a real opponent in my life. An instructor robot programmed for Je-kan-ia had been my teacher. But a robot's programming would be no match for a knight skilled in the use of Chamrah weapons.

Fflqa-Tur stepped into the arena. The crowd around us fell into an expectant silence. I looked around. Was Mother watching me now? I hoped she was. If she was, what was she thinking? I would have given anything to know. Here I stood, in the arena facing Fflqa-Tur – and even now it felt as if I was failing her. If only I'd left my Peacemaker alone – how much easier it would've been.

Fflqa-Tur raised his weapon and started moving towards me. Immediately, instinctively, I backed away, raising my sword between us. Fflqa-Tur and I circled warily around each other. My heart was about to explode from my chest. I could hear the blood roaring and rushing in my ears like a stormy sea. Fflqa-Tur lunged at me. Too terrified to even cry out, I leapt back. Staring at him, I took a deep breath, then another. Then I relaxed my grip on the sword. I'd been holding it so tightly that my fingers were turning numb.

Slowly I stood up straight. I'd made up my mind. I might lose, but Fflqa-Tur would know he'd been in a fight!

The battle between us lasted longer than I thought it would – a good 45 seconds at least. That wasn't the only surprise.

I won.

Heart pounding, head throbbing, palms sweating, I won. My first two moves stopped Fflqa-Tur's attempts to lunge at me. With my third sword stroke, I knocked his weapon out of his hand. It sailed up into the air away from us. I thrust forward until the point of my sword was against Fflqa-Tur's body. He didn't say a word. No one around us moved. The silence was deafening. I watched him, he watched me. Then I threw my sword down on to the ground.

I waited anxiously, unsure what to do next.

There was a long pause. Then, without warning, Fflqa-Tur tilted his head back and laughed – or rather, he did what had to be the Chamrah equivalent. The others around the arena joined in, until the air was filled with their laughing.

'Is that it?' I asked, confused. 'What happens now?'

'Well done, little one. You have passed our test.'

'Test?'

'You accepted my challenge. You fought, but you did not kill,' said Fflqa-Tur.

'Test?' Then I realized. 'You let me win! But ... but I could have killed you.' I stared at him.

Fflqa-Tur beckoned to one of his crew. The crew member left his seat and came into the arena. He picked up the weapon I had just thrown on the ground. Before I could stop him, before I could even cry out, he lunged at Fflqa-Tur. I watched, wide-eyed with horror as the sword blade passed right through Fflqa-Tur's body. The captain didn't even flinch. In fact he laughed again at the look on my face.

Then I saw what had happened. All the canals filled with grey liquid and one of Fflqa-Tur's hearts had moved out of the way of the sword. They had all shifted to be either above or below the blade.

'Every part of me has a life of its own,' explained Fflqa-Tur. 'And they could see the sword coming.'

'But I don't understand. Why this test?' I said slowly, trying to take it in.

'We Chamrah have to choose our friends carefully. We are a peaceful race. We do not want aggressors as friends. Nor do we want aggressors using our trade routes. But we do not want cowards as our friends either. You showed that you were prepared to fight for what you believed in, no matter what the outcome – but you didn't kill me. You could have done but you didn't,' said Fflqa-Tur.

'Because killing is wrong,' I said.

'Then why did you accept the challenge?' Fflqa-Tur asked.

'Because ... because it seemed to me that sometimes ... sometimes you have to take a stand, even if you know you're going to lose.' I frowned. 'And I couldn't let you destroy our ship and kill all those people, not when I thought I could do something about it. How could I sit back and not do something about it?'

'You are indeed very brave,' said Fflqa-Tur. 'And bravery is everything.'

Bravery ... would Mother see it that way? But then a strange thought occurred to me. By refusing to kill, but not running away, didn't Mother do exactly what I was doing now? In her own way, Mother was just as brave as Fflqa-Tur. Only I'd never realized it before.

'Can they still see me on the *Kitabu*?' I asked.

'Yes.'

I turned to the viewer. 'Mother, I need to see Doctor Bevan. I did recode my Peacemaker, but don't worry. I won't tamper with it any more.'

'Peacemaker?' said the captain.

So I explained.

Fflqa-Tur said, 'But you have proven that you do not need to wear such a device. You were prepared to fight and die for your ship and your comrades, but you weren't prepared to kill needlessly. You showed compassion. That was all we needed to see.'

I looked down at my Peacemaker ... and wondered.

'I will escort you to my bridge. You will be sent back to your ship from there,' said Fflqa-Tur.

As we walked back, I turned to the captain and said, 'Fflqa-Tur, may I keep my weapon and armour? As a souvenir?'

Fflqa-Tur nodded. 'Will you be punished when you return to your ship?' he asked.

'I should think so,' I sighed. Thoughts of the essays I'd

have to write and the endless lectures I'd have to listen to filled my head.

'Is there no one on your ship who will be proud of you?' asked Fflqa-Tur.

'I ... I don't know.' I shrugged.

Somehow ... somehow I thought that Mother would understand. But even if she didn't, it wouldn't matter.

'I'm proud of myself,' I said at last. 'And that's enough.'

Virtually True

Paul Stewart

Sebastian Schultz. It isn't the kind of name you come across every day. But there it was, large and clear, at the top of the newspaper article in front of me.

The reader of the newspaper was a big woman with heavy shoes, black tights and a tartan skirt. I couldn't see her face, but I could hear her wheezy breath.

MIRACLE RECOVERY, the headline said. *Sebastian Schultz, a 14-year-old schoolboy from South London, awoke yesterday from a coma that doctors feared might last for ever.* After that, the words got too small to read.

Sebastian, I thought. Sebastian Schultz. It couldn't be the Sebastian Schultz I'd met. That wouldn't be possible. But seeing the same name in the paper was a helluva coincidence. I leant forward to read the rest of the article.

Six weeks ago, schoolboy Sebastian Schultz was badly injured in a motorway accident. His condition, on arrival at the General Hospital, was described as critical though stable. Despite doctors' hopes, however, the boy did not regain consciousness. His parents, June and Ted Schultz, were informed that their son was in a coma.

At a press conference this morning, Mr Schultz admitted, 'That was the news we had been dreading.'

'You always pray it won't happen to you,' his wife added. 'We knew that the doctors were doing all they could, but in our hearts we knew we needed a miracle.'

Now that miracle has happened ...

At that moment, the woman shifted round in her seat, and her hand moved down the page. I suddenly saw the photograph that went with the story, and gasped. Although the boy in the picture was younger than the Sebastian I'd met, there was no doubt. They were the same person.

'But how?' I muttered.

'A-hem!' I heard, and looked up. Two beady black eyes were glaring at me from above the paper.

'I'm sorry, I ... '

But the woman was not listening. Turning the page noisily, she laid the newspaper down on her lap – so I wouldn't be able to see the back, I suppose – and went on reading.

It didn't matter, though. I'd already seen all I needed to see. Sebastian Schultz, the boy I'd got to know so well recently, had apparently been in a coma for all that time. I felt nervous and shivery. It didn't make any sense. It didn't make any sense at all.

I sat back in my seat, stared out of the train window and ran through the events in my head. The more I remembered, the crazier the situation seemed to be.

It all started a month ago. Dad and I had spent the entire Saturday afternoon at the Rigby Computer Fair.

Dad's nutty about computers. He's got a Pentium 150 Mhz processor, with 256MB of RAM, a 1.2GB hard disk drive and 16 speed CD ROM, complete with speakers, printer, modem and scanner. It can do anything. Paint, play music, create displays – even when my homework's rubbish, it *looks* fantastic. If I could just get it to make the bed and fold up my clothes it would be perfect.

Best of all are the games. *Tornado, Megabash, Scum City, Black Belt, Kyrene's Kastle* – I've played them all. With the screen so big, and the volume up loud, it almost feels as if you're inside the games, battling it out with the *Zorgs, Twisters, Grifters*, or whatever.

Of course, Dad was never satisfied. Technology was advancing every day, and he couldn't resist any of the new gadgets or gizmos that came on the market.

That was why we went into Rigby for the Computer Fair. After hours of looking at what was on offer, we came away with a virtual reality visor and glove, and a handful of the latest interactive psycho-drive games. They're terrific. Not only do the visor and glove change what you see, but better than that, you can control the action by what you're *thinking*. Well cool!

When we got them, I thought the games were all new.

Now, I'm not so sure. In fact I remember now that one of them had some brown spots on the plastic cover which I scraped off with my finger nail.

Anyway, back at home, Dad set everything up. I plugged myself in, switched on and launched myself off into the first of the games. It was called *Wildwest*.

That's what I like about computers. The more futuristic they get, the better you can understand the past. I wasn't standing in the converted loft – the Powerbase, as Dad calls it – any more. I was really there, striding down the

dusty track through the centre of town. There was a sheriff's badge pinned to my shirt.

As I burst in through the swing-doors of the saloon, everyone went silent and loads of shifty pairs of eyes turned and glared at me. I strode over to the bar – nonchalantly. 'Sarsaparilla!' I said and a glass of fizzy red stuff came sliding along the bar towards me. As I took a sip, a piano began playing and the conversation started up again.

Suddenly, I heard a loud crash behind me. I spun round. There, silhouetted in the doorway, was Black-Eyed Jed, the fastest gun in the west. 'This town ain't big enough for the both of us, Sheriff Dawson,' he drawled, and fingered his guns lightly. 'Let's see what you're made of, boy,' he sneered. 'Outside. Just you and me.'

I can remember grinning. This was *really* cool!

'You'll be smiling on the other side of your face when I've finished with you, Sheriff,' said Black-Eyed Jed.

I finished my drink and slammed the glass down on the bar. Jed had already left the saloon. All eyes were on me once again as I walked calmly back across the room. A man's gotta do what a man's gotta do, I thought happily, and wondered what sort of score I was notching up.

All at once, something strange happened. Something

really strange. Up until that point, the game had been pretty much as I expected. But when the *second* sheriff appeared through the back door, shouting and waving his arms about, I realized that the game was more complicated than I'd thought.

'Don't go out!' the second sheriff shouted.

'And who are you? This town ain't big enough for the two of *us*,' I quipped.

'I'm serious,' the sheriff cried, and I knew he meant it.

'Who *are* you?' I said again. He wasn't like the other characters in the saloon. For a start, he was younger – about my age – and although he looked like a computer image, he somehow didn't move like one.

'There's no time to explain,' he shouted. 'Just follow me.'

I did what I was told. I'm not sure why. We raced down a corridor, and through a door. The room was full of smoke and men playing cards. We ran past them, and out through another door. A woman screamed, and hid herself behind a full-length mirror. As we walked by, I stopped and waved at my reflection.

Clever, I thought.

'Come ON!' shouted the other sheriff.

We went on through another door, and another, and another – and ended up back in the saloon.

'NO!' screamed the second sheriff. Then he ran to the back of the saloon and dived through the window. By the time I had climbed out after him, he was already sitting on a horse. 'Jump up!' he cried.

He kicked the horse, and we sped off in a cloud of dust.

'Who are you?' I asked for a third time.

But the second sheriff still didn't answer. He'd seen the posse of men on horseback speeding after us. 'Keep your head down,' he said.

At that moment, the sound of a gunshot echoed round the air. The second sheriff groaned, and his body slumped back against me. Ahead of me, in bright neon lights across the sky came a message.

GAME OVER.

As I slipped off the visor, the empty desert disappeared and I found myself back in the Powerbase. I took off the glove and headphones. My head was still echoing with the sound of the firing gun. I glanced at the score on the screen. 21,095. Then I noticed something else.

While I'd been in the Wild West, the printer had come on. I picked up the piece of paper from the tray.

At the top was a picture of the second sheriff. This time, though, he was wearing jeans, sweatshirt and trainers. Printed over the bottom of the photograph was a name. *Sebastian Schultz – 23 January 1985 – ?* Below it, a message: I'M STUCK. PLEASE HELP TO RETRIEVE ME. TRY 'DRAGONQUEST'. .

Of course, I wanted to go straight into the game he'd suggested, but it was already half an hour after lightsout, and I didn't want Mum to have some reason for keeping me off the computer. Sebastian and *Dragonquest* would have to wait.

The next morning, I was up and back on the computer

before the milkman came. By the time his float jangled and clinked its way along our street, I'd already walked through the massive studded doors of the dragon's castle lair.

The aim of the game was simple. I had to rescue the fair Princess Aurora from the wicked dragon, and collect as much of the creature's treasure along the way as I could. I'd already got loads of stuff by the time I reached the princess, who'd been imprisoned at the top of a tall tower. She was a young woman with incredibly long golden plaits.

'My hero!' she squealed. 'Take me away from all this.' Behind me, I could hear the dragon roaring as it pounded up the stairs. 'Make haste, my brave knight,' the princess said urgently. 'Rescue me now.'

'Never mind her,' came a voice, and a second knight appeared from the wardrobe. 'It's *me* who needs rescuing!'

'Fie! Pish! And fooey!' the princess complained. 'I'm the damsel in distress here, not you!'

The dragon was getting closer.

'Sebastian?' I said.

The second knight nodded. 'Quick,' he said. 'While there's still time.' And with that, he did something which really wasn't very gallant, considering he was meant to be a knight. He pulled out a huge pair of scissors and chopped off the princess's two long plaits. Then he tied them together, fixed one end round the bedpost and threw the other end out of the window.

'NOW!' he screamed, as he leapt for the window and disappeared from view down the hair rope.

At that moment, the dragon – a huge great scaly slobbering beast – appeared at the doorway. I gasped, and leapt for the window after Sebastian. As I lowered myself down I felt the dragon's fiery breath on my fingers.

Across the moonlit battlements we ran, down a spiral staircase, across a banqueting hall, and through a secret passage on the other side of a tapestry. And the whole time I could hear and feel and even *smell* the evil dragon following in close pursuit.

'The dungeons,' Sir Sebastian cried out. 'They're our only hope.'

We went down the cold stone steps, swords drawn. The cries of imprisoned men, women and children filled the chilly damp air. Suddenly, the dragon appeared at the end of the corridor. Massive it was, with teeth the size of daggers and claws like carving knives. It was fast, too, despite its size. Before we even had time to turn around, the dragon was on us.

I swung my sword. I parried and thrust. But it was no good. The dragon was only interested in Sebastian, and there was nothing I could do to prevent it getting him.

GAME OVER.

This time, the message in the printer was a little longer. BETTER LUCK NEXT TIME. LET'S HOPE IT'S THIRD TIME LUCKY, EH? PLEASE DON'T GIVE UP ON ME, MICHAEL. OTHER WISE I'LL HAVE TO STAY LOCKED UP IN HERE FOR EVER. TRY 'JAILBREAK'. I THINK IT MIGHT JUST WORK! CHEERS, SEB.

I didn't even bother to read the rules of *Jailbreak* before going in. I knew that whatever the computer said, *my* task would be to rescue the boy. And sure enough, my cell mate was prisoner 02478: Schultz.

'I've got to get out of here,' Sebastian sighed. 'Are you going to help?'

'Of course I am,' I said. 'Have you got a plan?'

Stupid question. With the help of a skeleton swipe-card, we were soon out of the cell and racing down corridors. Sirens wailed, guard dogs howled, heavy boots came tramping. Behind us, steel-barred doors slammed shut, one after the other. We dodged the guards, we fled the dogs, we made it to a staircase and pounded upwards.

On the roof, Sebastian looked round at the horizon and glanced at his watch nervously. 'It should be here by now.'

'What?' I said.

'That!' said Sebastian and pointed. I saw a small dot in the sky, and heard a distant *chugga-chugga*, which was getting louder by the second.

'A helicopter!' I exclaimed.

'That was *my* idea!' said Sebastian excitedly. 'If only it would go a bit faster ... '

At that moment, the door behind us burst open. Twelve guards with twelve vicious dogs were standing there. As I watched in horror, the guards bent down and unclicked the dogs' leads. The next instant they were hurtling across the roof towards us, all bared teeth and dripping jowls. Out of the corner of my eye, I saw Sebastian take a step backwards.

'NOOOOOO!' I screamed.

But it was too late. The boy had slipped from the roof and was already tumbling back through the air, down to the concrete below.

GAME OVER.

As I removed the visor, I looked in the printer tray. This time it was empty. I felt really bad. I'd failed Sebastian; I'd failed the game. It was only later, when the scenes began to fade in my memory, that it occurred to me that Sebastian Schultz *was* the game.

Strangely, though, although I went back to *Wildwest, Dragonquest* and *Jailbreak* after that, I never met up with Sebastian again. Dad said it must have been a glitch, but I wasn't convinced.

Then, yesterday, I heard from Sebastian again. It was Wednesday, and I'd got home early from games. I went straight up to the Powerbase and there, in the printer tray, was a sheet of paper.

CAN WE HAVE ONE LAST TRY? it said. I THINK THE HELICOPTER WAS THE RIGHT IDEA, BUT ESCAPING FROM A PRISON WAS WRONG. THERE'S GOT TO BE SOME KIND OF AN ACCIDENT ... GO

INTO 'WARZONE'. IF THIS DOESN'T WORK I WON'T
BOTHER YOU AGAIN. CHEERS, SEB.

I couldn't tell which war zone we were in. Basically, it was
a city somewhere. The tall buildings were windowless and
riddled with holes. Machine-gun fire raked the sky. Walls
tumbled. Bombs exploded. All I knew was that Sebastian
and I had to make it to that helicopter in one piece.

Heads down and arms raised, we ran across a no-man's-
land of rubble and smoke, dodging sniper fire as we did
so. At the far end we went through a door in a wall. The
helicopter was on the ground about three hundred metres
away, propeller a blur, waiting for our arrival.

We started to run, but the tank fire sent us scuttling
back to the wall.

'A Jeep,' Sebastian shouted to me, and nodded at a
camouflage-green vehicle parked by the road. 'Just what
we need!'

'I can't drive,' I said.

'Neither can I,' said Sebastian. 'But we've got no other choice.' He jumped in, turned the ignition key and revved the engine. 'Jump in!'

I climbed into the passenger seat, and we were off.

'Uh oh,' said Sebastian, glancing in his mirror. 'There's a tank behind us.'

I spun round. The tank was hurtling along after us at a terrific speed. Not only did we have to go like maniacs, but Sebastian had to keep swerving this way and that to avoid the shells being fired at us.

Suddenly, with the helicopter only ten metres away, Sebastian slammed on the brakes and sent the Jeep skidding into a spin. I leapt clear, scrambled up and jumped into the waiting helicopter.

'Made it!' I said. The helicopter immediately started to go upwards. I looked around. Sebastian wasn't there. 'Wait!' I shouted at the pilot.

I looked back. The Jeep had stopped, but Sebastian hadn't got out. The tank was bearing down on him.

'COME ON!' I yelled. But Sebastian didn't move. Sitting staring at the oncoming tank, it was as if his body had been turned to stone.

All at once, the air was filled with the sickening crunch of metal on metal as the tank crashed into the side of the Jeep. I saw Sebastian's face fill with panic and confusion as he was thrown up out of his seat and into the air.

Round and round he tumbled, over and over – closer and closer to the helicopter. He landed with a thud on the ground, just below the hatch. I leant down quickly, grabbed him by the wrist and pulled him up.

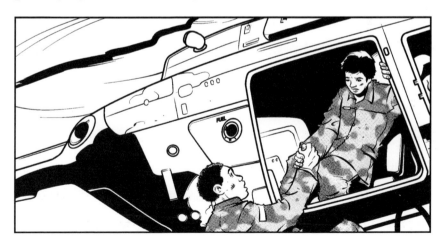

Not a moment too soon. As he sat down beside me, the helicopter soared up into the sky.

I'd done it. I'd rescued Sebastian at last. Before I had a chance to say anything to him though, the helicopter flew into thick cloud. It poured in through the open door and turned everything blinding white. I couldn't see a thing – until 'GAME OVER' flashed up.

When I removed the visor, the screen was flashing a score of 40,000,000.

Forty million! I'd hit the jackpot. I'd finally cracked the game.

At least, that was what I thought then. Now I knew that Sebastian Schultz, the boy from the game, really did exist. I'd seen the proof in the newspaper.

But how? I wondered as I got off the train. What was going on?

Questions, I had plenty of. It was time for some answers. Home at last, I raced up to the Powerbase and checked the printer. There was nothing there waiting for me. Feeling a bit miffed, I went into the Net instead. I wanted to learn more about the MIRACLE RECOVERY story.

I found what I was looking for quickly enough – and there was far more there than in the woman's newspaper. It was on page two that something interesting caught my eye. As I read on, my head started reeling.

Apparently, at the time of the accident, Sebastian was using his laptop to play one of the same psycho-drive games that I've got.

My heart pounded furiously. I felt hot and cold all over. What if ... ? No, it was too incredible ... But the thought would not go away.

What if, because Sebastian had been plugged into the computer when he'd banged his head in the accident, the computer had saved *his* memory in its own? And if that was the case, then what if the weird versions of the games *I'd* been drawn into – *Wildwest* and *Dragonquest, Jailbreak* and *Warzone* – had all been attempts to retrieve that memory?

After all, what's it Dad's always saying about the

computer's memory? 'It can never forget, Michael. Nothing ever gets lost.'

The thing is, I thought, even if it was somehow possible that Sebastian's memory had been stored on disk, then how had it ended up on *my* computer? Scrolling down the article, I discovered a possible explanation on the final page.

Answering a reporter's question as to what the family was going to do next, Mr Schultz said that they were off to DCL Computers to stock up on some games. 'It was while we were in the hospital. Someone broke into the car and stole the lot. I don't know what happened to them'.

'I do,' I said quietly. 'They ended up at the Computer Fair. And *we* bought them.'

Having finished the article, I left the Net and checked my e-mail. There were two letters. One from my uncle David in New York. And one from Sebastian.

Of course, I thought. It was stupid of me to expect a letter in the printer tray. How could there have been?

Sebastian had escaped. With trembling fingers I clicked in, and read the message.

DEAR MICHAEL, it said. THANK YOU! I'M NOT REALLY SURE HOW IT HAPPENED – EITHER (?), BUT THANKS. YOU SAVED MY LIFE. LET'S MEET UP SOME TIME SOON. WE NEED TO TALK – BUT DON'T MENTION ANY OF THIS TO ANYONE ELSE. IT'LL ONLY FREAK THEM OUT. CHEERS, SEB. P.S. KEEP THE GAMES. YOU'VE EARNED THEM.

I shook my head in amazement. A real message from the real Sebastian Schultz. Even though he didn't understand it any more than I did, we both knew that by reliving the accident, *something* had happened. Something weird, something wonderful – something that should have been impossible. But then again, as Dad says, 'Now that there are two advanced intelligences on earth, who can say what is and what isn't possible?'

All I know is this. Everything that I've described is true. Virtually.

Moving House

Louise Cooper

I shouldn't have done it. I really shouldn't. But it's too late to be sorry now.

Mum and Dad had decided to move home, so I went along with them to look at a house. It was an old house, and it hadn't been lived in for a while. I liked it, especially when I saw that it had a cellar. Well, there was this door under the stairs – it had to lead to a cellar, didn't it? But when I tried to open it, it was locked.

'Oh,' said the estate agent, 'there's no cellar. It was filled in. The door's sealed up, and there's just solid brick behind it.'

He took Mum and Dad into the kitchen. But I stayed behind. That door looked so *interesting*. I was certain there must be *something* behind it.

Then I saw a rusty key hanging by the door.

And sure enough, when I tried it in the cellar door, it fitted. The door wasn't sealed up at all. As soon as I turned the key it creaked open, and behind it ... *Yes!* There was a flight of steps vanishing into darkness. Of course, I went down them. Down and down. They seemed to go on forever. And they kept turning, and twisting, until I was ...

Lost.

Oh, yes; lost. Because when I turned round, there were the steps behind me. Only they led *downwards*, not back up. I looked for steps that went up, but there weren't any.

'Mum?' I called. 'Dad?'

No one answered.

'Help!' I shouted.

But no help came.

I don't know how long I've been down here. It must be ages, because I'm much taller, and I've got a long beard. My clothes don't fit me now, but I can't get any more.

I have food, though, because there are lots of rats and spiders here. And when it rains outside – wherever 'outside' is – water trickles down the walls, so I get enough to drink. But I wish someone would come. They must have tried to find me. Why haven't they? Maybe the steps have got something to do with it. Because whichever direction I turn, there they are. Always leading *down*.

So if you ever find a key to a door that people say can't be opened because there's nothing there ...

Well, don't pick that key up. Just *don't*. Right?

Nule

Jan Mark

The house was not old enough to be interesting, just old enough to be starting to fall apart. The few interesting things had been dealt with ages ago, when they first moved in. There was a bell-push in every room, somehow connected to a glass case in the kitchen which contained a list of names and an indicator which wavered from name to name when a button was pushed, before settling on one of them: *Parlour; Drawing Room; Master Bedroom; Second Bedroom; Back Bedroom.*

'What are they for?' said Libby one morning, after roving round the house and pushing all the buttons in turn. At that moment Martin pushed the button in the front room and the indicator slid up to *Parlour*, vibrating there while the bell rang. And rang and rang.

'To fetch up the maid,' said Mum.

'We haven't got a maid.'

'No, but you've got me,' said Mum, and tied an old sock over the bell, so that afterwards it would only whirr instead of ringing.

The mouse-holes in the kitchen looked interesting, too. The mice were bold and lounged about, making no effort at all to be timid and mouse-like. They sat on the draining board in the evenings and could scarcely be bothered to stir themselves when the light was switched on.

'Easy living has made them soft,' said Mum. 'They have a gaming-hell behind the boiler. They throw dice all day. They dance the cancan at night.'

'Come off it,' said Dad. 'You'll be finding crates of tiny gin bottles, next.'

'They dance the cancan,' Mum insisted. 'Right over my head they dance it. I can hear them. If you didn't sleep so soundly, you'd hear them too.'

'Oh, that. That's not mice,' said Dad, with a cheery smile. 'That's rats.'

Mum minded the mice less than the bells, until the day she found footprints in the frying-pan.

'Sorry, lads, the party's over,' she said to the mice, who were no doubt combing the dripping from their elegant whiskers at that very moment, and the mouse-holes were blocked up.

Dad did the blocking-up, and also some unblocking, so that after the bath no longer filled itself through the plug hole, the house stopped being interesting altogether; for a time.

Libby and Martin did what they could to improve matters. Beginning in the cupboard under the stairs, they worked their way through the house, up to the attic, looking for something; anything; tapping walls and floors, scouring cupboards, measuring and calculating, but there were no hidden cavities, no secret doors, no ambiguous bulges under the wallpaper, except where the damp got in. The cupboard below the stairs was full of old pickle jars, and what they found in the attic didn't please anyone, least of all Dad.

'That's dry rot,' he said. 'Thank god this isn't our house,' and went cantering off to visit the estate agents, Tench and Tench, in the High Street. Dad called them Shark and Shark. As he got to the gate he turned back and yelled, 'The Plague! The Plague! Put a red cross on the door!' which made Mrs Bowen, over the fence, lean right out of her landing window instead of hiding behind the curtains.

When Dad came back from the estate agents he was growling.

'Shark junior says that since the whole row is coming down inside two years, it isn't worth bothering about.

I understand that the new bypass is going to run right through the scullery.'

'What did Shark senior say?' said Mum.

'I didn't see him. I've never seen him. I don't believe that there is a Shark senior,' said Dad. 'I think he's dead. I think Young Shark keeps him in a box under the bed.'

'Don't be nasty,' said Mum, looking at Libby who worried about things under the bed even in broad daylight. 'I just hope we find a house of our own before this place collapses on our heads – and we shan't be buying it from the Sharks.'

She went back to her sewing, not in a good mood. The mice had broken out again. Libby went into the kitchen to look for them. Martin ran upstairs, rhyming:

'Mr Shark,
In the dark,
Under the bed.
Dead.'

When he came down again, Mum was pulling away the sewing and Libby was parading around the hall in a pointed hat with a veil and a long red dress that looked rich and splendid unless you knew, as Martin did, that it was made of old curtains.

The hall was dark in the rainy summer afternoon, and Libby slid from shadow to shadow, rustling.

'What are you meant to be?' said Martin. 'An old witch?'

'I'm the Sleeping Beauty's mother,' said Libby, and lowering her head she charged along the hall, pointed hat foremost, like a unicorn.

Martin changed his mind about walking downstairs and slid down the banisters instead. He suspected that he would not be allowed to do this for much longer. Already the banister rail creaked, and who knew where the dreaded dry rot would strike next? As he reached the upright post at the bottom of the stairs, Mum came out of the back room, lugging the sewing-machine, and just missed being impaled on Libby's hat.

'Stop rushing up and down,' said Mum. 'You'll ruin those clothes and I've only just finished them. Go and take them off. And you,' she said, turning to Martin, 'stop swinging on that newel post. Do you want to tear it up by the roots?'

The newel post was supposed to be holding up the banisters, but possibly it was the other way about. At the foot it was just a polished wooden post, but further up it had been turned on a lathe, with slender hips, a waist, a bust almost, and square shoulders. On top was a round ball, as big as a head.

There was another at the top of the stairs but it had lost its head. Dad called it Ann Boleyn; the one at the bottom was simply a newel post, but Libby thought that this too was its name; Nule Post, like Ann Boleyn or Libby Anderson.

Mrs Nule Post.

Lady Nule Post.

When she talked to it she just called it Nule.

The pointed hat and the old curtains were Libby's costume for the school play. Martin had managed to stay out of the school play, but he knew all Libby's lines by heart as she chanted them round the house, up and down stairs, in a strained, jerky voice, one syllable per step.

'My-dear-we-must-in-vite-all-the-fair-ies-to-the-chris-ten-ing, Hello, Nule, we-will-not-in-vite-the-wick-ed-fair-y!'

On the last day of term, he sat with Mum and Dad in the school hall and watched Libby go through the same routine on stage. She was word-perfect, in spite of speaking as though her shock absorbers had collapsed, but as most of the cast spoke the same way it didn't sound so very strange.

Once the holidays began Libby went back to talking like Libby, although she still wore the pointed hat and the curtains, until they began to drop to pieces. The curtains went for dusters, but the pointed hat was around for a long time until Mum picked it up and threatened, 'Take this thing away or it goes in the dustbin.'

Libby shunted up and down stairs a few times with the hat on her head, and then Mum called out that Jane-next-door had come to play. If Libby had been at the top of the stairs, she might have left the hat on her bed, but she was almost at the bottom so she plonked it down on Nule's cannon-ball head, and went out to fight Jane over whose turn it was to kidnap the teddy bear. She hoped it was Jane's turn. If Libby were the kidnapper, she would have to sit about for ages holding Teddy to ransom behind the water tank, while Jane galloped round the garden on her imaginary pony, whacking the hydrangea bushes with a broomstick.

The hat definitely did something for Nule. When Martin came in later by the front door, he thought at first that it was a person standing at the foot of the stairs. He had to look twice before he understood who it was. Mum saw it at the same time.

'I told Libby to put that object away or I'd throw it in the dustbin.'

'Oh, don't,' said Martin. 'Leave it for Dad to see.'

So she left it, but Martin began to get ideas. The hat made the rest of Nule look very undressed, so he fetched down the old housecoat that had been hanging behind the bathroom door when they moved in. It was purple, with blue paisleys swimming all over it, and very worn, as though it had been somebody's favourite housecoat. The sleeves had set in creases around arms belonging to someone they had never known.

Turning it front to back, he buttoned it like a bib round

Nule's neck so that it hung down to the floor. He filled two gloves with screwed-up newspaper, poked them into the sleeves and pinned them there. The weight made the arms dangle and opened the creases. He put a pair of football boots under the hem of the housecoat with the toes just sticking out, and stood back to see how it looked.

As he expected, in the darkness of the hall, it looked just like a person, waiting, although there was something not so much lifelike as deathlike in the hang of those dangling arms.

Mum and Libby first saw Nule as they came out of the kitchen together.

'Who on earth did this?' said Mum as they drew alongside.

'It wasn't me,' said Libby, and sounded very glad that it wasn't.

'It was you left the hat, wasn't it?'

'Yes, but not the other bits.'

'What do you think?' said Martin.

'Horrible thing,' said Mum, but she didn't ask him to take it down. Libby sidled round Nule and ran upstairs as close to the wall as she could get.

When Dad came home from work he stopped in the doorway and said, 'Hello – who's that? Who ... ?' before Martin put the light on and showed him.

'An idol, I suppose,' said Dad. 'Nule, god of dry rot,' and he bowed low at the foot of the stairs. At the same time the hat slipped forward slightly, as if Nule had lowered its head in acknowledgement. Martin also bowed low before reaching up to put the hat straight.

Mum and Dad seemed to think that Nule was rather funny, so it stayed at the foot of the stairs. They never bowed to it again, but Martin did, every time he went upstairs, and so did Libby. Libby didn't talk to Nule any more, but she watched it a lot. One day she said, 'Which way is it facing?'

'Forwards, of course,' said Martin, but it was hard to tell unless you looked at the feet. He drew two staring eyes and a toothy smile on a piece of paper and cut them out. They were attached to the front of Nule's head with little bits of chewing-gum.

'That's better,' said Libby, laughing, and next time she went upstairs she forgot to bow. Martin was not

so sure. Nule looked ordinary now, just like a newel post wearing a housecoat, football boots and the Sleeping Beauty's mother's hat. He took off the eyes and the mouth and rubbed away the chewing-gum.

'*That's* better,' he said, while Nule stared once more without eyes, and smiled without a mouth.

Libby said nothing.

At night the house creaked.

'Thiefly footsteps,' said Libby.

'It's the furniture warping,' said Mum.

Libby thought she said that the furniture was walking, and she could well believe it. The dressing-table had feet with claws; why shouldn't it walk in the dark, tugging fretfully this way and that because the clawed feet pointed in opposite directions? The bath had feet too. Libby imagined it galloping out of the bathroom and tobogganing downstairs on its stomach, like a great white walrus plunging into the sea. If someone held the door open, it would whizz up the path and crash into the front gate. If someone held the gate open, it would shoot across the road and hit the district nurse's car, which she parked under the street light, opposite.

Libby thought of the headlines in the local paper – NURSE RUN OVER BY BATH – and giggled, until she heard the creaks again. Then she hid under the bedclothes.

In his bedroom Martin heard the creaks too, but he had a different reason for worrying. In the attic where the dry rot lurked, there was a big oak wardrobe full of old dead ladies' clothes. It was directly over his head. Supposing it came through?

Next day he moved the bed.

The vacuum cleaner had lost its casters and had to be helped, by Libby pushing from behind. It skidded up the hall and knocked Nule's football boots askew.

'The Hoover doesn't like Nule either,' said Libby. Although she wouldn't talk to Nule any more she liked talking *about* it, as though that somehow made Nule safer.

'What's that?' said Mum.

'It knocked Nule's feet off.'

'Well, put them back,' said Mum, but Libby preferred not to. When Martin came in he set them side by side, but later they were kicked out of place again. If people began to complain that Nule was in the way,

Nule would have to go. He got round this by putting the right boot where the left had been and the left boot on the bottom stair. When he left it, the veil on the hat was hanging down behind, but as he went upstairs after tea he noticed that it was now draped over Nule's right shoulder, as if Nule had turned its head to see where its feet were going.

That night the creaks were louder than ever, like a burglar on hefty tiptoe. Libby had mentioned thieves only that evening, and Mum had said, 'What have we got worth stealing?'

Martin felt fairly safe because he had worked out that if the wardrobe fell tonight, it would land on his chest of drawers and not on him, but what might it not bring down with it? Then he realized that the creaks were coming not from above but from below.

He held his breath. Downstairs didn't creak.

His alarm clock gleamed greenly in the dark and told him that it had gone two o'clock. Mum and Dad were asleep ages ago. Libby would sooner burst than leave her bed in the dark. Perhaps it *was* a burglar. Feeling noble and reckless he put on the bedside lamp, slid out of bed, trod silently across the carpet. He turned on the main light and opened the door. The glow shone out of the doorway and saw him as far as the landing light switch at the top of the stairs, but he never had time to turn it on. From the top of the stairs he could look down into the hall where the street light opposite shone coldly through the frosted panes of the front door.

It shone on the hall-stand where the coats hung, on the blanket chest and the brass jug that stood on it, through the white coins of the honesty plants in the brass jug, and on the broody telephone that never rang at night. It did not shine on Nule. Nule was not there.

Nule was half-way up the stairs, one hand on the banisters and one hand holding up the housecoat, clear of its boots. The veil on the hat drifted like smoke across the frosted glass of the front door. Nule creaked and

came up another step.

Martin turned and fled back to the bedroom, and dived under the bedclothes, just like Libby who was three years younger and believed in ghosts.

'Were you reading in bed last night?' said Mum, prodding him awake next morning. Martin came out from under the pillow, very slowly.

'No, Mum.'

'You went to sleep with the light on. *Both* lights,' she said, leaning across to switch off the one by the bed.

'I'm sorry.'

'Perhaps you'd like to pay the next electricity bill?'

Mum had brought him a cup of tea, which meant that she had been down to the kitchen and back again, unscathed. Martin wanted to ask her if there was anything strange on the stairs, but he didn't quite know how to put it. He drank the tea, dressed, and went along the landing.

He looked down into the hall where the sun shone through the frosted glass of the front door, on to the hall-stand, the blanket chest, the honesty plants in the brass jug, and the telephone that began to ring as he looked at it. It shone on Nule, standing with its back to him at the foot of the stairs.

Mum came out of the kitchen to answer the phone and Martin went down and stood three steps up, watching Nule and waiting for Mum to finish talking. Nule looked just as it always did. Both feet were back on ground level, side by side.

'I wish you wouldn't hang about like that when I'm on the phone,' said Mum, putting down the receiver and turning round. 'Eavesdropper. Breakfast will be ready in five minutes.'

She went back into the kitchen and Martin sat on the blanket chest, looking at Nule. It was time for Nule to go. He should walk up to Nule this minute, kick away the boots, rip off the housecoat, throw away the hat, but ...

He stayed where he was, watching the motionless football boots, the dangling sleeves. The breeze from an open window stirred the hem of the housecoat and revealed the wooden post beneath, rooted firmly in the floor as it had been for seventy years.

There were no feet in the boots; no arms in the sleeves.

If he destroyed Nule, it would mean that he *believed* that he had seen Nule climbing the stairs last night, but if he left Nule alone, Nule might walk again.

He had a problem.

Acknowledgements

The publishers gratefully acknowledge permission to reproduce the following copyrighted material:

The Glass Cupboard © Terry Jones, 1981. First published in *Fairy Tales* by Terry Jones, (Anova Books, 1981).

Water, Water, Water and **Thank Goodness!** © Michael Rosen, 1988, 1994. First published in *Fantastically Funny Stories* by Michael Rosen (Kingfisher, 1994).

The Balaclava Story © George Layton, 1975. First Published in *The Fib and Other Stories* by George Layton (Pearson Education Limited, 1975).

Peacemaker © Malorie Blackman, 1999. First published in *Peacemaker and Other Stories* by David Belbin, Malorie Blackman, Tony Bradman and Nicholas Fisk (Pearson Education Limited, 1999).

Virtually True © Paul Stewart, 1997. First published in *Sensational Cyber Stories* by Tony Bradman (Random House, 1997).

Moving House © Louise Cooper, 2002. First published in *Short and Scary!* by Louise Cooper (Oxford University Press, 2002).

Nule © Jan Mark, 1980. First published in *Nothing to be Afraid of* by Jan Mark (Kestrel Books, 1980).

Every effort has been made to contact copyright holders of material reproduced in this book. Any omissions will be rectified in subsequent printings if notice is given to the publishers.

Illustrations in this edition by Neil Chapman, Mike Phillips, Pete Smith and Nigel Dobbyn.